Christmas Magic

Book 6 in the series
Chronicles of the Southern Thirties

Christmas
Magic

A Story for Children

BETTY B. LEVIE
LOUISE B. NOLEN

Illustrations by Judith Jordan

The Pea Pod Tree Publishing Company
P.O. Box 288
Fayette, AL 35555

Books in the series, *Chronicles of the Southern Thirties*, depict the life of a middle-class Southern family during the perilous years of the Great Depression.
Young readers can learn about Alabama's past as they follow the small-town adventures of Whitson Brooks, his wife Nona, and their three children, Louise, Betty and Thomas.

ISBN 0-9638776-4-X

Produced for the
Pea Pod Tree Publishing Company
by the Black Belt Press of Montgomery, Alabama. Design by Randall Williams.

To Our Children

and Grandchildren

With Love

T he bell rang. School was out for a whole week. Christmas holidays had begun.

As the children filed out of the large, old, two-story brick building, Louise stopped at the end of the sidewalk. She had to wait on her younger sister and brother, Betty and Tommy. Mama had told her to be sure that she had both of them with her before she started for home.

Louise was so excited that she could hardly stand still. The magic of Christmas was everywhere! Her mind replayed the wonderful events of the day. The whole school had gone to the big assembly hall and listened to Mr. Beck, the principal, who read from the big Bible about the story of Jesus. They had sung beautiful Christmas carols that Louise loved. Back in the classroom, Mrs. Sams had given out drawings of Christmas trees to color and decorate. For dinner that day, Mama had packed a nice surprise for Louise. There in her lunch bag were three large tea cakes decorated with red stars. Louise shared them with her best friend, Jean Riley. After dinner,

the class had gathered around the large cedar tree in the corner of the room. It was decorated with paper ornaments that the children had made. Mrs. Sams gave out the presents that were under the tree. Louise's gift was three "Big Little Books." She was thrilled. One book would have been enough, but to get three was just wonderful. Hands had pulled at Louise's skirt as Betty and Tommy tried to show her their gifts. Betty's gift was a tiny baby doll that moved. Tommy's gift was a tin race car with wheels that really rolled.

No wonder the day at school had made Louise so happy.

She took the children's hands and started down the sidewalk in the direction of home. As they turned the corner at Mackey's Service Station, Tommy pulled his hand free from Louise and started to run.

Louise called out, "Tommy, you better slow down! You remember what Mama said."

Tommy didn't stop; he just ran down the sidewalk toward his friend Charles Houston, who was sitting by the side of the road. When Tommy reached him they began roughhousing. Before long, the frolicking really became rough. Charles Houston bumped Tommy's nose and the trouble really started. Everyone knew that Tommy's nose would bleed at the least bump. This time was no different. As the bleeding grew worse, Tommy rolled Charles Houston over on his back. He held his arms down, sat on him, and let his nose bleed all over Charles Houston's face. Charles Houston wiggled, squirmed, and tried to get up, but could not.

Louise yelled, "Tommy, stop that!"

The girls ran. Betty reached the boys first. She grabbed the nape of Tommy's shirt and pulled him off Charles Houston. Then she pinched his nose tightly to stop the flow of blood. Meanwhile, Louise began to wipe Charles Houston's face with her little white handkerchief.

"Are you hurt, Charles Houston?" asked Louise.

"No!" he yelled, jerking his arm loose. He took off, running up the sidewalk toward his house.

Louise turned and looked at Tommy. Blood was everywhere, all down the front of his white shirt, on his hands and face, and all over his pants. "Mama is gonna wear you out when you get home!" she shouted.

All was quiet as they headed for home. They walked past the big Methodist church on their left, and then the big Baptist church on their right. Louise loved that beautiful Baptist church with its large stained-glass windows. She could hardly wait for Sunday to come. The family would all attend church. In Sunday school, they would have more gifts, candy, and carols. Oh, the magic of Christmas! Louise felt like running.

By this time, the children had reached the big highway that ran between Ashland and Lineville. It had been paved last summer. They remembered sitting on the grass in front of the house watching the men as they worked.

They walked on down the side of the big road. The sidewalk ended and they were careful to watch for cars. Before long, the sidewalk began again. It ran in front of five houses that were near their home. Tommy yelled, "Step on a crack, break your mama's back!" Of course, the girls laughed and made sure they didn't step on a crack.

At last it was time to cross the highway. Louise looked both ways. No car could be seen. The children ran across the highway and through the apple orchard into the yard.

Mama was in the kitchen washing dishes from the day's baking. She had baked two Christmas cakes. One was a delicious fruit-filled Japanese cake. The other was Daddy's favorite. It was a luscious three-layered burnt caramel. Mama had wrapped each cake in a clean, white flour sack. Then she stacked them in a five-gallon lard can. Mama put the can on the back porch to keep the cakes cool. Every day she would pour some of her sweet scuppernong wine over the Japanese fruit cake. This made the cake moist. As Mama was drying her hands she heard the front door open. The children rushed into the house. Mama met them at the kitchen door.

"My, my," laughed Mama. "What's all this?" The children tried to hug Mama and show gifts at the same time. Then Mama saw the blood all over Tommy. "Mama, Tommy got into a fight with Charles Houston. He let his nose bleed all over Charles Houston's face," said Louise.

"I'll tend to you later, young man," said Mama sternly. "Go wash your face and hands."

"Come now," said Mama, as Tommy returned to the kitchen. "Sit down and have some milk and some of my fresh tea cakes. Tell me about your day at school."

Mama opened the ice box and took out a large, blue pitcher filled with cold sweet milk. She stirred the milk with a long wooden spoon. The stirring mixed the thick, yellow cream throughout the milk. Then Mama poured the sweet milk into three sparkling glasses. She set the glasses in front of the children. The children were quiet for a little while as they ate the Christmas cookies and sipped the cold milk. Then they began chatting happily and telling Mama all about their day.

Mama hated to end the fun, but she finally reminded them it was time to do their chores.

Tommy walked slowly to the big pile of stove wood in the back yard. He began filling his arms with the wood. Trudging back and forth to the kitchen, he filled the big wooden box by the iron stove with short sticks of wood. He hoped that this Christmas Santa would bring the red wagon he had asked for. He could really use it for hauling wood.

Meanwhile, the girls picked up the slop bucket. It was filled with dish water and leftover food from the day. They started for the hog pen, carrying the bucket between them. As they drew near, the hogs began squealing, grunting, and running toward the trough. "Just like hogs," thought Louise, as the hogs began rooting each other out of the way. Each hog was trying to be first to get to the trough. The girls poured the slop into the trough and set the bucket down. Then they headed for the barn to feed the other animals.

Louise opened the crib door slowly. She didn't want the big barn rats to jump out at them. But when she saw two large tabby cats sitting on a pile of corn, switching their tails and watching for rats, Louise knew all was well. No rats would be around for a while.

The girls shucked about thirty big yellow ears of corn. They put the shucks in a basket for the cows. The ears were placed in a large basket for the horse and mule. Before long, the mule was chomping corn in his stall and the girls turned toward the stall where their wonderful horse, Lady, was kept. The scent of hay from the stall caused the girls to feel warm all over. The girls stood in front of Lady and gave her an evening meal of sweet feed and corn. They rubbed her soft velvet nose with their hands. They really loved that beautiful reddish-brown horse.

The sun set as the girls carried the rest of the shucked corn to the hogs. Then they picked up the slop bucket and walked slowly back to the house.

The girls returned to the kitchen, washed their hands and began to set the table for supper. Tommy was playing with his new car under the table. He stared hungrily at the big iron stove where Mama was busy

cooking. Dried black-eyed peas and hog jowl were boiling in a pot on the back of the stove. Hot corn bread was baking in the oven, and Mama was frying salmon patties in a black iron skillet. At the sound of the car, Mama looked out the window. Daddy was home for supper.

The children were so tired from their exciting day at school that they ate their supper, washed their feet, and went straight to bed.

Saturday passed uneventfully. The children spent the day helping Mama clean the house for Christmas.

Sunday arrived cloudy and warm. The family, dressed in their best clothes, climbed into the car and drove to church. Church that day was as wonderful as Louise had expected it to be. She sensed Christmas magic again.

After dinner, Daddy announced that he was ready to cut a tree. The excited children yelled, "Wait for us," and bounded up the stairs to dress in their old clothes.

It was a happy group that headed for the woods behind the house. They trooped up hills, down hollows, and across branches, looking for just the right cedar tree.

As the group climbed a small hill, Daddy stopped. He whispered, "Look!" Then he pointed to a tall pine tree on his right. The children looked. There on the side of the tree sat the largest woodpecker they had ever seen.

"That's an ivory-billed woodpecker," said Daddy. "We called it an 'Indian hen' when I was a boy. There are not many of them left." They watched the beautiful bird.

Tommy began to chant:

"Red head peckerwood

"Sittin' on a pine,

"Wants a chew tobacco

"But you can't chew mine."

Betty joined in the chant and soon they all were chanting and laughing. Suddenly everyone stopped as if a spell had been cast on them.

There, on the top of the hill between two large pines, was the most beautiful cedar tree the children could imagine. The sun suddenly broke through the clouds and it seemed to shroud the tree with a holy light. A hush hung over the entire woods. Then the children came to life and started running. They were yelling and laughing as they circled the tree. The children looked for a blemish, but none could be found.

Daddy arrived with the ax. "Is this the one you want, kids?"

"Oh yes!" answered the children. The air was filled with the scent of cedar chips as Daddy chopped down the wonderful tree. Daddy threw the tree over his shoulder and the group started for home.

The journey was very pleasant, but tiring. When they reached home, Mama had hot chocolate and more delicious Christmas tea cakes ready for them to enjoy. Everyone was full of excitement and eager to tell Mama all about their

19

adventure. When the chocolate and tea cakes were gone, Mama had the children lie down on the living-room rug to rest. They were soon fast asleep.

About an hour later the children were aroused from their peaceful sleep. The smell of cedar filled the house. Daddy was placing their beautiful tree in its special place of honor, the front corner of the living room.

At that very moment, Mama came in with a large box of decorations for the tree. She had had some of the decorations since her first Christmas with Daddy. Every year she added something new. This year, it was a string of lights she had ordered from the Sears and Roebuck mail-order catalog. The children sat back on their haunches to watch Mama and Daddy string the lights on the tree. When they finished, the children jumped up to help Mama place the ornaments on the tree. There were colored bells, glass pine cones painted different colors and frosted with snow, and celluloid wise men riding camels. There were silver celluloid angels and a beautiful gold celluloid star for the top of the tree.

Last of all, the family hung silver icicles on almost every needle of the tree. The tree seemed to be shrouded in silver protecting the fragile glass ornaments.

Louise and Betty unwrapped a soft, stuffed Santa from his folds of white tissue paper. He was dressed in gold lamé, trimmed in white fur. The girls placed him by the side of the fireplace to welcome the real Santa.

As the children stepped back to view their handiwork, Mama whispered, "Watch the new lights," and turned them on.

The children watched the tree with awe. The lights made every object on the tree seem to come to life. Everything was blinking, glittering, shining, shimmering, and glowing. The new lights seemed to be boiling. They were round at the bottom like a half-ball with a tube coming up out of the middle. As they became warm, big bubbles ran up  and down the tube. Mama had outdone herself this time. The new lights were just like magic.

"Just like magic," thought Louise. There it was again, the magic of Christmas!

Louise woke early the next morning. Sounds from the kitchen were drifting up the stairwell into the bedroom. The sun was shining and Louise knew it would be another warm day. She wished it would turn cold so Daddy could kill the hogs. She had heard Mama tell Daddy that the meat was about gone. She was worried.

Louise slipped quietly out of bed. She dressed quickly and tiptoed down the hall and stairs. As Louise entered the kitchen, Mama was sitting at the table cutting out circles from brown paper bags. She would use them to line the bottom of the big iron skillet, to keep the cakes from sticking when she baked them. Louise sat down and told Mama she would wait on the others to eat her breakfast. She wanted this time to talk to Mama.

Louise and Mama discussed everything from school to hog killing. Mama put Louise's worry over the household meat shortage to rest. She told her that Daddy would kill the hogs even if the weather didn't cooperate. They could always hang the hogs in the town ice house until it did turn cold. With that worry settled, Louise ventured to tell Mama that some of her little friends were saying that there was no Santa Claus. Mama assured her that as long as she believed in Santa, he would continue to visit her.

About that time, the two younger children, laughing and pushing each other, rushed into the kitchen for breakfast. While the children ate, Mama was busy getting ready the things she needed for baking cakes.

She took a big coconut from the icebox. Then she hammered a large nail into the eyes of the coconut to make holes. Next she poured out the sweet, white milk into a bowl. Mama would use the milk in making the icing for her coconut cake. She held the coconut tightly in her hand and cracked it with the hammer. She gave the coconut several hard taps. It split into many pieces. She then gave a piece to each child. They took case knives and pried the meat from the shell. Mama peeled the brown hull from the white coconut as the children handed the pieces to her.

Louise and Betty grated the coconut. The grater was a metal box with a handle at the top. Each side had perforations with the sharp ends of metal protruding. The children would rub the coconut meat over the sharp edges to make it soft and fine. They tried hard not to grate their knuckles. If they got blood in the white coconut, Mama would just dip it out with a spoon. But, oh, how their knuckles would hurt.

By the time the coconut was grated Mama was ready to beat the cake. She sat in a straight-backed, cane-bottomed kitchen chair. She placed the mixing bowl between her knees.

She had placed one-half pound of soft, sweet butter in the bowl to mix with two cups of sugar. Mama used her hand to mix the sugar and butter. She squeezed the batter with her fingers until it was smooth and creamy.

Betty and Louise added the other ingredients as Mama needed them. Then the beating really began. Mama cupped her hand and started beating that batter. Mama's beating sounded like the loud clopping noise of a horse trotting. Louise and Betty watched and laughed. They could hardly wait to lick the bowl. Mama always left batter in the bowl for the children to enjoy.

While the cake layers baked, the girls were sent to clean the upstairs bedrooms. They made up the beds, swept the floors, and picked up any clothes or toys left lying around. By the time the cake was done, the girls were back in the kitchen helping Mama get dinner ready.

There sat the cake, in all of its white coconut glory, ready to be wrapped and placed in the lard can on the back porch with the other Christmas cakes.

That afternoon Mama and the girls baked a three-layered chocolate cake with pecans on top. It too, was wrapped in a soft flour sack and placed in the lard can.

Christmas Eve arrived dark, warm, and raining. It poured all morning, but by afternoon it had slowed to a drizzle.

Daddy took the car and drove the children to town. They were going to do their Christmas shopping for the family. Daddy dropped the children off at Adam's Drug Store, where they purchased four small blue

bottles of Evening in Paris perfume. From there, they walked to the five-and-ten-cent store to purchase gifts for each other. They were to meet Daddy in one hour at Levie's grocery store on the corner.

At Levie's, they would purchase their gifts for the men in the family—Prince Albert pipe tobacco for Papa Jackson, and Mickey Twist chewing tobacco for Daddy.

That night Mama ironed the wrapping paper left over from last Christmas. Then she and the children wrapped the gifts and placed them under the tree. Louise felt the tree glowed even more with Christmas magic.

Stockings had to be hung from the mantel. The children hurried to their parents' bedroom. They returned with the longest socks they could find in Daddy's drawer. A nail was hammered through the top of each sock into the wooden mantel above the fireplace. The children were now ready for a visit from St. Nick.

As the children sat on the floor of the living room at Mama's feet, she began reading in her soft, Southern voice the story of "The Night Before Christmas." After Mama's story, Daddy picked up the Bible and finished reading the wonderful Christmas story of Jesus's birth. Then he laid the Bible back on the table. This signaled the children that it was time for bed. They kissed Daddy and started up the stairs.

A tired, excited, and nervous group of children all climbed into one bed. They always slept together on Christmas Eve. Mama heard their prayers and kissed each one good night. Then she turned out the light.

Tommy went to sleep quickly, but the girls lay there listening to the rain and wind. They whispered and talked about Santa. They were too excited to sleep.

Louise knew that if Santa heard them talking, he wouldn't come, but

she wanted to hear him come tonight to satisfy her mind.

They had been whispering for quite a while, when a sudden terrible sound was heard on the roof.

"Santa Claus!" they both whispered. They knew he must have landed on the roof with his reindeer. Quick as lightning, they covered their heads with the quilt and held their breath and didn't move.

Louise was startled out of a sound sleep. Something or someone had grabbed her arm. Her heart was beating wildly. Was it Santa or one of his elves?

Betty whispered, "Louise, you awake?"

"You scared me half to death," said Louise.

"Is it time to get up?" asked Betty.

"I'll see," answered Louise. She climbed out of bed and turned on the light. The small clock on the dresser showed 4:55. Yes, it was time to get up.

Louise realized it had turned cold in the night and the rain had stopped.

Louise and Betty dressed hurriedly, each putting on a heavy sweater. The girls woke Tommy and helped him dress. Louise hurried down the hall to his room to get his coat. Quietly, the children crept down the hall. The stairs creaked as they stepped on each tread. The sound was as loud as a gunshot to their ears. When they reached the bottom of the stairs, Louise told the two younger children to wait while she went to wake Mama and Daddy.

Betty and Tommy sat on the second step. The fires had burned out during the night and the house was cold. They huddled together for warmth and security. They were scared that Santa might not have visited them.

Louise rushed down the hall praying that Santa had come. As she reached her parents' bedroom, she heard their heavy breathing and thought they were still asleep.

Louise leaned over and whispered hoarsely in Mama's ear.

"Mama, wake up. It's Christmas."

Mama opened her eyes, smiled, and grabbed Louise. Hugging her

close, she said, "Christmas gift!"

Daddy ruffled her hair and called out, "Christmas gift!" They had gotten Louise this time.

"Go back with the young ones. We'll be there shortly," said Mama. Louise slipped back to the stairs and sat huddled with the others.

Presently, they heard Daddy stoking the fire in the big furnace in the basement. Heat began to fill the hall and stairs and the children felt warmth and peace settling over them.

Mama and Daddy came down the hall, laughing and talking. "Do you reckon the old fellow came?" laughed Daddy.

Mama walked into the living room and plugged in the Christmas tree lights. The room sprang to life. "Santa Claus did come!" laughed Mama. "Just come and see."

The children jumped off the step and rushed to the doorway, where they stopped and from that distance surveyed the wondrous things Santa had brought. There under the Christmas tree were all the things the children had asked for and much more. There was Tommy's red wagon filled with all kinds of surprises. There were toy trucks and race cars, a toy gun with a holster, and coloring books with crayons.

As Louise and Betty peered at their gifts, they saw baby dolls and wooden trucks filled with clothes for each doll. There sat a real, little electric stove with pots and pans. There, by the side of the tree, was a beautiful blue tea set. There were more coloring books with crayons.

Their stockings were bulging with goodies. They pulled out apples,

oranges, coconuts, hard candy, and all kinds of nuts. Lying on the table was a box of large dried grapes still clinging to the vine.

Louise felt the Christmas magic all around her. It seemed to fill the very insides of her until she could hardly breathe.

Mama and Daddy watched the children enjoying their gifts from Santa and they were filled with pride and love. Then Mama rose from her chair to go prepare breakfast.

Daddy announced that he had to get the hen ready for Mama to cook for Christmas dinner. Tommy went with him, pulling his new red wagon. As they reached the back yard, the sun was beginning to make its way up in the east. Daddy saw that it would be a beautiful, clear, cold day.

As Tommy watched, Daddy walked to the garage. He took the fat hen out of the chicken coop. Holding the hen by its head, Daddy began to wring its neck, swinging it round and round. The head came off in his hand and the body fell to the ground where it flopped and flopped in the dirt, slinging blood everywhere.

Daddy walked back to the house to get a pot of boiling water. When he returned to the yard, he pushed the hen down into the scalding water. Scalding made the feathers easier to remove. He plucked every feather, making the hen appear naked. Then he flung the feathers and water into the weeds at the edge of the yard. As he turned back toward the house, the fox hounds set up their yelping and barking until Daddy strolled down to the pen. Jumping up on the fence, the dogs began licking Daddy's

hands. He rubbed their heads and promised to take them hunting next Saturday night.

Daddy carried the hen into the kitchen for Mama to finish dressing while he milked the cow.

When Mama cut the hen open, she found several small, round, yellow balls that would have become eggs. The hen had been a good layer, but now it would be a good dinner. Before long, the hen was bubbling away in the big pot on the back of the stove.

When Daddy returned with the milk, Mama strained it, washed the straining cloth, and hung it on the back porch to dry. Daddy brought canned food up from the basement. Soon the food was cooking in other pots on the big stove.

Around eleven o'clock, Mama paused in her cooking long enough to change her apron and smooth her hair. It was almost time for Papa Jackson and family to arrive.

Mama walked into the living room to check on the children. The girls had dressed in their best dresses and Tommy had on his Sunday pants and shirt. Mama combed the girls' hair while Tommy was sent to wash his face and hands. She had no sooner finished with the girls' hair when she heard a car drive up. The family had arrived.

There was much hugging and kissing and calling out "Christmas gift!" Gifts were placed by each plate on the dining table, to be opened before eating the Christmas dinner.

Papa Jackson followed the children into the living room to see what Santa had brought, while Miss Fanny, Mary Lou, and Ada went to the kitchen to help Mama get the dinner on the table.

Everyone "oohed" and "aahed" over their gifts. Daddy's gift was a box of Mickey Twist chewing tobacco. Papa Jackson received his usual tin of pipe tobacco. Miss Fanny, Mary Lou, Ada, and Mama, really liked their Evening in Paris perfume in the beautiful little blue bottles. The children's gifts were large two-layer boxes of chocolate-covered cherries.

After Daddy returned Grace, every one began eating Christmas dinner. Oh, what a table full of food.

The hen rested in front of Daddy, surrounded by wonderful cornbread dressing, with the giblet gravy nearby. There were mashed potatoes, creamed corn, candied yams, green beans, English peas, sweet pickles, dill pickles, tomato relish, candied crabapples, green onions, and Mama's store-bought cranberry sauce. On the sideboard were huge plates of sliced cakes and a big bowl of ambrosia.

Louise was so glad that Mama didn't make the children wait until the adults had finished eating.

As always, Christmas dinner was a great success. Papa Jackson pushed back his chair, sighed, and said, "That was the best Christmas dinner I have ever eaten— bar none." Everyone smiled because Papa

Jackson always said that about any dinner he ate. But on this occasion, everyone agreed with him. Daddy, the children and Papa Jackson retired to the living room to let their meals settle while the ladies cleared the table and washed the dishes.

After an enjoyable afternoon, Papa Jackson announced that it was time for his family to start for home. When the good-byes were over, the children asked if they might walk up the street to see what their friends had received from Santa. The parents agreed, but said they must be back by dark.

When Louise said her prayers that night, she was very thankful for the Lord Jesus being born on Christmas, and for Santa Claus, who had proven himself real again. Then she thanked the Lord for the cold weather and for the wonderful Christmas magic that seemed to cover her like a blanket.

As Louise closed her eyes she felt peaceful and secure in her own wonderful little part of the big world.

Sisters Louise Nolen (left) and Betty Levie have transformed their love of the South and their recollections of their childhoods into a series of books set in Alabama during the Great Depression. For older readers, they hope their stories prompt warm memories; and for younger readers, they hope to bring understanding of experiences that shaped earlier generations.

BETTY B. LEVIE was born in Eustis, Florida, and grew up in a small, rural Alabama town during the Depression years. She earned a B.S. degree in biology and an M.S. degree and a teaching certificate from Jacksonville State University, and a reading specialist certificate from Auburn University. She lives in Ashland, Alabama, and is married to Paul G. Levie; they have two daughters and two granddaughters.

LOUISE B. NOLEN was born in Coleta Valley in Clay County, Alabama, and as a child lived in Eustis, Florida, before her family moved back to Ashland, Alabama. She earned the B.S. degree from the University of Alabama, and has an honorary doctorate from Livingston State University. She was married to the late Charles W. Nolen; they have four daughters, two sons, and thirteen granddaughters. She lives now in Fayette, Alabama.